Thoughts of Erotica

Joe Brock

D1527653

Thoughts 1-20

§

Thought 1

It was midnight, cold and dark as my car raced down the winding mountain road and as I sensed being closer to home it was almost as if I could feel your body calling out to me.. Like your voice was somehow whispering in my ear, as if you could sense me too the closer I drew near.. I loosened the knot in my tie and tugged at my collar a little as my thoughts of you provoked the animal inside me and I began to sweat.. Time seems to slow down as the voice of you grows louder in my ear and echoes in my head, visions of you replace the winding road in my eyes and I flash into a dream, seeing you standing there waiting for me as I get home.. As the door closes behind me and I drink you in with my eyes you slowly approach.. Just before I open my mouth to speak you place a finger on my lips and silence me.. Running your hands along my body you slowly unbutton my shirt and take of my belt.. Sliding your hand down my pants to feel my cock throbbing between my legs, and as you massage it for me feeling it grow larger in your hand, you hold my hands above my head and kiss my neck driving me absolutely wild.. Until I can take no more and I break free of your grip, grabbing you by your ass and lifting you up into my arms and wrapping your legs around my waist.. You run your fingers through my hair and kiss my lips deeply sending chills through my spine.. For a second my knees become weak and it feels as though we might fall and you just bite my lip gently and tighten your grip in my hair and suddenly my strength restores and I feel stronger than I've ever been.. Carrying you into the bedroom and tossing you down on the bed, you undo your bra strap and expose your perfectly shaped, round perky breasts and my eyes instantly become fixated on your light brown nipples slowly growing stiff and becoming erect as you lick your finger tips and begin to tease them.. Biting your lips and watching me stand over you and disrobe myself completely, my rock hard cock standing fully at attention for you just waiting for the chance to pleasure you and slide up deep inside you.. As you look back up into my eyes, glance back down again, then back up and smile just a bit still biting your lips I can't help but jump on top of you and begin to ravish your body.. Kissing, licking and sucking my way from your legs and inner thighs, up around your navel and stopping for a moment or two at your breasts, taking your nipples in my mouth flicking them a few times with my tongue as I bite down on them softly between my teeth.. Every time I do your grip on my hair tightens a little more and you wince in pain and pull my hair causing me to moan for you.. Feeling myself begin to throb between your legs the head of my cock just inches from your dripping wet pussy, feeling the heat and sweat dripping off our bodies.. As I buried my face between your neck I spread your legs apart with my knees and with one hand I guided my stiff cock just inside your pussy just teasing you with the head.. Holding your throat with my other hand and leaning in to kiss your lips I slowly forced myself all the way inside you until you had taken every inch as deep as I could go.. Throwing your hands back gripping the pillow and head board and flexed your legs as your hips rocked back and forth matching the rhythm of my strokes.. As I continued to pound your pussy your moans they turned to screams and you shouted out my name as if it was your safe word and I was just ignoring it.. Over and over you moan and scream for me as your wrap your arms around my neck and dig your nails into my back, into my flesh making me go harder to compensate for the pain.. It seemed the more you hurt me the more pleasure you received.. And as you run your fingers down my back and leave scratch marks as your trail, I push your legs back further bending your knees forcing them to touch your chest.. Your ankles wrapped around my neck and your toes beginning to curl behind my head.. As I continue to increase my strokes and fuck you harder and harder I look down into your eyes, I like to watch and see the pleasure on your face.. You tell me exactly when you are ready to cum as you struggle to maintain your eye contact with me but as you begin to lose control those eyes slowly start to roll back in your head and your body starts to shake.. Your legs they tremble and your pussy clenches down tight around my cock as I continue to thrust in and out of you even as your body convulses and you explode and cum.. Your hands gripping the back of my head pulling my hair and pulling me down to kiss your lips and as we kiss your moans still manage to slip out.. With one final thrust I pull out and just when you thought you were finished cumming you experience what feels like a second explosion between your legs and you release one more time squirting out what seems like a gallon of cum.. Soaking my body and the sheets in your sweet juices.. And just as you finish you look up at me in pure disbelief and just fall back almost fainting on the bed, your heart racing and out of breath.. When all of a sudden the room starts spinning and time no longer feels slow, I snap back into reality and my vision of you is replaced once again with the winding road as I find myself still racing home to you, the dream.. It was all just a dream.. My thoughts, they felt so real..

§

Thought 2

She was beautiful.. Stunning, as she sat across the bar from me in the darkest corner, lights flickering across her face and somehow her eyes remained illuminated even in the shadows.. They were piercing, as if she was looking straight through my soul.. I knew she saw me looking at her but she wasn't looking away and neither could I, as I sipped my drink our eyes just remained locked on each other.. I could feel her exploring my soul, her fingers tapping on the bar but not to the rhythm of the music playing, instead she was matching the beat of my heart.. She smiled when she saw me notice, as if she knew I just figured out her secret.. She kicked back her head taking down the last of her drink like a shot, as I did the same.. I called the bartender over and gave him payment for my tab as well as hers.. I took my spare hotel key and scribbled my room number on it with the pen I used to sign my bill, as I stood up and walked toward her our eyes once again remained locked on each other.. No words were spoken, no names exchanged, both of us trying to look deeper Into the others soul.. I took her hand and folder her fingers over my room key as I placed it in her palm.. Gave her a quick wink as I let go and smiled, bowed my head down to her and turned to walk away.. I made my way up to my room, walking slowly through the lobby admiring the sophisticated decor, watching everyone bustle around living their own lives and adventures.. Then I remembered the girl from the bar again all of a sudden, she snapped back into my mind immediately and took over complete control of my thoughts.. I was distracted by nothing and no one else as I quickly caught the next elevator and hit the button for the 47th floor.. It seemed like the longest ascent in an elevator I had ever experienced in my life, the stress of watching the numbers slowly go up, making several stops along the way, had caused little beads of sweat to form on my brow.. Finally as the numbers turned from 46 to 47 and the bell rang and the doors open time froze.. Everything happened slower than slow motion and it was almost as if the doors were opening to a room much brighter than it was supposed to be.. As I blinked my eyes once or twice the doors finally became open enough to reveal a silhouette standing in the light.. As I took a few steps forward and out of the elevator time snapped back into real motion and the bright light faded away, I rubbed my eyes quick and they reopened to see the girl from the bar, standing with her hand on her hips, biting her lips and smiling just a bit.. She was holding the key to my room, turning it between her fingers, she looked down at it for a moment then shifted her gaze to the throbbing bulge forming in my pants and finally locked her eyes with mine once more.. She took my hand and lead me speechlessly to my room, opening the door and then closing and locking it behind us, hanging a do not disturb sign on the outer knob.. As she turned and faced towards me again she placed her hand on my chest and pushed me gently and as she took a step forward I took one backward.. We reach the edge of the bed and just before I'm about to fall back she grabs my face and kisses me deeply, my arms wrap around her waist and pull her in close to me.. It felt like a spark of electricity between us, as if she had found a way to plug herself into me and we felt the rush of energy and power over take our bodies.. She jumped up to wrap her legs around my waist and I gripped her thighs tightly, turning around to face the bed I laid her down slowly, gently on her back.. Kissing her for a few more moments and as I pull away she bites on my bottom lip.. Our eyes closed for a second and as we both breath deep and time slows down, the only sound that can be heard is the pounding of heart beats.. I stand up to remove my clothes quickly pulling my shirt over my head and dropping my pants down to kick them off.. By the time I've finished she's already lying naked with her arms back with one finger by her lips as if she is biting her nail while her eyes explore my body and mine begin to drink her in.. I grab her legs and pull her body down closer to me, picking her up to her knees and pulling her into me I kiss her lips once more, eager to feel that rush of energy again.. Our naked bodies meeting each other for the first time, skin to skin and sweat beginning to drip.. As we kiss I reach my hand down between her legs and before I even begin to touch and tease her she is already wet.. Dripping in fact, as I slide a finger inside just to flick her throbbing clit, her body catches a chill and shivers run up her spine.. I remove my hand and lay her down once more gently on her back.. Kiss my way up her body from her thighs, to her stomach, to her

10

chest.. Biting on her chin softly and then resting my face in her neck, kissing and sucking on that spot that drives all women insane.. She wrapped her arms around my head and pulled my hair a little bit, and she whispered in my ear.. "Give it to me baby, give me that dick.." My body trembles at the sound of her voice, chills running through me as though there were ice in my veins.. As I spread her legs apart and forced myself between her thighs I lifted her legs up just a bit and bent her knees, sliding my way inside her dripping wet pussy.. Still sucking on her neck her hands still locked behind my head, she was moaning and biting my ear as I thrust myself slowly in and out of her.. She begun to beg for it harder, faster.. She dug her nails into my back and whispered in my ear once more.. "Make me cum for you, please baby make this pussy cum for you.." Before she finished her sentence I raised up and looked her dead in her eyes, reaching down to grab her by her neck I lifted her legs all the way back and begun to pound her pussy just the way she asked for it.. Her moans became screams the harder I fucked her and she threw her hands down to grip and pull the sheets.. Her feet up on my shoulders one hand gripping her left thigh the other hand firmly around her neck, she was desperately trying to look into my eyes but with every stroke I hit it deeper and she couldn't keep her own from rolling back in her head.. She bit her lip and a look of confused pleasure began to creep onto her face, at the same time her legs begun to tense up and I felt the pressure build up throughout her body just begging her to release.. She started to shake and scream out in ecstasy and she finally let go, exploding and cumming like she had never felt before.. Her entire lower body shaking and convulsing as I continued to thrust and stroke in and out of her drenched pussy, cum dripping down her thighs and staining the sheets.. As she twitched and tensed up one final time and all of her cum had been drained from her body I felt her relax, her legs became heavy on my shoulders as she sunk into the bed, I slid out from between her and let them fall to the bed with the rest of her body, I walked around the bed side she was closest to and rested one knee beside her head and let her taste herself off my cock as she moaned with pleasure.. I ran my fingers through her hair and kissed her softly on her head, excused myself to the bathroom to take a quick shower and clean off while she caught her breath.. I took a five minute shower and emerged back into the room.. Drying my face with a towel and when I looked up she was gone, the bed was made everything was put back in place.. The only thing out was a half empty bottle of gin with a single shot glass on the table.. There were no traces of her, no clothes, no note.. Nothing.. Was she real?? Had I imagined that whole thing in a drunken stupor?? My mind was spinning as I collapsed onto the bed, my vision grew blurry and everything faded to black as I drifted off into my dreams..

§

Thought 3

As the handle turns at the flick of your wrist and the hot water starts pouring down onto your body you feel a slight chill, a shiver run down your spine as you feel my breath on your neck.. Your hairs stand up on edge and goose bumps rise on your skin even as the scolding water fills the entire bathroom with steam.. My fingers begin to tease and trace the outlines of your every curve, as I stand behind you and suck on your neck I slide my hand around your hips and between your legs.. Feeling your warm wetness dripping from your pussy as I gently slide a finger up inside you and flick your throbbing clit.. Your arms slowly reaching up to grab my head as you lean back to kiss my lips, the water raining down on your perfect breasts.. I turn you towards me and force your back up against the wall, taking one leg in my hand and raising it up, the other hand planted firmly on your neck.. As I kiss you deeply I feel you reach down and take my swollen cock in your hand to guide me inside of your tight pussy.. As you maneuver the head of my throbbing dick between your thighs I slowly begin to slide the tip in and out, just teasing you a bit.. As I pull away from you and bite your outstretched lip I suddenly thrust myself inside you, giving you every inch all at once.. Forcing myself as deep as I can possibly go until it feels as though I'm deep enough to touch your soul.. As I stroke and pound your pussy continuing to slam you up against the wall, still gripping tightly on your throat and leg still lifted off the ground.. You moan for me wrapping your hands around me one gripping my hair the other around my back, nails digging deep into my skin.. You whisper in my ear begging me to make you cum, begging me to satisfy your cravings, all your sexual desires and needs.. I kiss you again pulling out, spinning you around once more to face the far wall I make you lean forward and put your hands above your head to brace yourself.. While I spread your legs apart I grip your waist with one hand as I guide my cock back inside of you with the other hand.. Slowly teasing you once more with just the tip, then all at once thrusting myself back inside you again while pulling your waist towards me going deeper than I've ever gone before.. Your moans become screams as you let my name slip from your lips as loud as ever, your voice echoing off the marble walls in the shower..

As I feel your body start to tremble and shake you keep one hand up on the wall to brace yourself and you reach the other behind your back as if you were being handcuffed, opening and closing it begging for me to reach out and take it.. So I grab your wrist with one hand and pull your arm back towards me, and with the other I reach up and grab your hair pulling your head back towards me.. With one final stroke I feel your legs tense up and you flex every muscle in your body as you explode for me.. Releasing all your cum as you let go and drown in ecstasy, your knees becoming weak you struggle to hold yourself up as I practically keep you from falling still gripping on your wrist and hair.. As you finish cumming and your body starts to relax you fall forward onto your arm still supporting yourself on the wall, your feet relax and you lower yourself from standing on your toes.. You collapse into the wall as I gently let you go, I move close to you and hold your body tightly kissing your lips while the water continues to fall and drench our bodies.. As you try to catch your breath I wash myself off and give you a wink as I step out of the shower.. I smile and blow you a kiss telling you to have a good day and I let you finish starting your morning..

§

Thought 4

I anxiously awaited your arrival at the train station, checking my phone every two seconds to see if the time had changed.. You came in on the 4:55pm train from Penn station out to the island to spend the night at my place.. Finally I see the lights of the train approaching through the clouds of my breath in the crisp November air.. As the train pulled into the platform and the doors open people came piling out there was an instant crowd, but there you were.. All bundled up in your hat and scarf, fly jacket and pants as always with some fresh kicks to match, pulling your head phones out of your ears and looking around for me.. I let you look for a few moments just watching you, taking you all in and enjoying the way you've caused my heart to suddenly beat faster, and finally you spot me.. Eyes locked and smiles instantly appear on our faces as I walk towards you and wrap my arms around you.. Hugging you so tightly just breathing you in, I always loved how your head fit just perfectly under my chin every time I embraced you.. Kissing the top of your head and then you look up at me with those beautiful eyes and that pretty smile.. For a second I don't speak I just smile back, and then I break the silence..

"Baby can I have my kiss hello please.." Biting my lip and looking down at you.. You can't help but laugh and give in closing your eyes and reaching close as our lips connect for the first time, it was like there was an electric charge that surged through our bodies as we kissed my grip tightened around you and you hugged even tighter around my waist with your arms.. Never in my life have I felt such a feeling with anyone, never have I felt such a connection from only a kiss, it was.. Incredible..

As we pull away you bite my lip just a bit and smile as you open your eyes again to look at me once more, as I look down on you I'm speechless.. I don't say a word I just wrap my arms around your shoulder and we walk off the train platform up the block to my apartment.. It's about a five minute walk and the entire time I just look down at you in complete amazement of how beautiful you are, I missed you so much I always hated how far apart we were.. No matter though because your here now and tonight you're all mine to take away from the world, if I had it my way I would just relive this night with you forever.. As we walk up the steps and get to my front door before I open it I pull you close and kiss you again, then bury my face in your neck and bite you just a little bit, right on the spot that drives you absolutely insane..

"Aye dio mios Joe not out here papi!" As you try not to smile and be all serious and get me off of you, but you can't help it, it just feels too good.. I know all your spots, I know all your weaknesses and you begin to melt in my arms, wrapping your arms around my neck and running your hands through my hair gripping tight and pulling it a little bit.. You start moaning for me as I push your back up against the door still kissing on your neck I lift one leg up and thrust my hips into you.. With my free hand I reach in my pocket for my keys and without moving my face from being buried in your neck I unlock the door and turn the handle holding you up so you don't fall back.. I quickly walk us inside and shut and lock the door behind us.. I was planning on cooking you dinner and watching a movie but I think we both agree at this point perhaps it would be best to just start with dessert.. As I pull away from you we both start stripping as fast as we possibly can, clothes go flying to every corner of the living room and as soon as we are both naked I tackle you to the floor.. Pinning your hands back to the floor locking our fingers and kissing you deeply, attacking your lips, both of us beginning to breath heavy, hearts starting to race.. My hands explore your body, every inch of you, my fingertips remembering your every curve, tracing your outlines and sending chills through your entire body, shivers down your spine.. As I begin to kiss my way around you moving from your lips to your neck and then down to your chest, teasing your nipples with my tongue and sucking on each of your breasts worshiping you.. Then beginning to lick my way down your navel stopping just above your pussy and then kissing my way around it, biting your inner thighs.. Putting my shoulder up underneath your legs to lift them up and spread them apart I bury my face between your legs, letting my tongue dive deep into your dripping wet pussy.. Flicking your clit, swirling it around in circles, first very slow and then very fast, sucking your pussy and nibbling on it ever so gently, softly biting down on your throbbing sensitive clit..

"Fuck Joe!! Shit!! Papi que Rico.." Screaming out for me as you grip my hair and pull my head around in between your legs making sure I get you from all the right angles.. I lick and suck your pussy until I just can't take anymore and I have to be inside you.. Lifting my head from between your legs but still keeping your legs on my shoulders I raised up to my knees and pushed yours back to your chest.. Leaning down to kiss you letting you taste yourself off my lips I reach my hand down to slide my throbbing cock into your dripping wet and ready pussy.. Even being so wet your still so tight I have to force my stiff cock all the way inside you forcing you to take every inch, once I'm all the way inside I begin to thrust my hips back and forth still kissing your lips.. Holding your hands above your head and pounding away at your pussy causing your body to rock back and forth, your breasts bouncing up and down to the rhythm of my hips.. I pull away from your lips and raise up to look down into your eyes, I feel your legs starting to twitch and your body beginning to shake, I like looking at your face when you cum.. So I reach down and grab your throat forcing you to look directly at me deep into my eyes, my other hand wrapped around one of your thighs and as I tighten my grip I give you one final deep stroke to finish you off.. Causing you to explode and release, screaming out my name as you cum for me.. Body twitching, legs shaking and muscles flexing, your pussy clenched down tight around my swollen cock still thrusting in and out of you slowly.. As you finish and you begin to let yourself relax, I kiss your legs as I let them fall from my shoulders down to the floor, kissing my way up your body until I reach your lips and give you a quick peck.. Your eyes closed, heart beating fast, desperately trying to catch your breath, you look so cute I can't help but smile and laugh.. I kiss you on your forehead and say..

"I missed you baby, I'm gonna make us dinner and then I want round 2.."

§

Thought 5

Walking out of the restaurant holding your hand in mine, feeling a little lightheaded from the glasses of wine I hand the valet my ticket and he goes to retrieve the car.. Pulling you in close to me looking down into your eyes my hand gripping firmly on your tight perfect ass, I lean down and kiss your lips becoming intoxicated even more with lust and temptation.. Fuck if I had it my way I rip your dress off and clear one of these table outside the restaurant and take you right here right now.. As you feel my heart beat pounding harder and faster on my chest you place your hands around my back and squeeze me tightly almost as if to say calm down, trying to tame the wild beast you know exists within me.. Just in time before I completely lose control the valet pulls up with the car, I reach down to open your door and hold your hand as you gently slide in.. Walking around to the driver side I hand the valet a $20 as he stands and waits for me to get in and close my door for me.. I look at you for a moment as I buckle my seat belt and put the car in gear, place my hand between your thighs and squeeze down tight and give you a wink as I hit the gas and go.. Speeding through the down town streets catching every green light never stopping once along the way we arrive at home just under 20 minutes later, music blasting and windows still down as we pull into the driveway and into the garage.. As I take the key from the ignition you lean over and kiss my lips whisper in my ear to meet you upstairs in 5 minutes and then nibble on my ear as you pull away and get out of the car quickly going into the house.. I get out of the car and lock up the garage and walk up the path to the front door, turning to close and lock it behind me and as I turn to go up the stairs I catch a glimpse of you standing at the top.. Stripped down to nothing but your boy shorts and one of my wife beaters with no bra on, your tits just hanging out freely I could see your erect nipples poking through.. Just standing there biting your lips with your hands on your hips looking down at me and just smiling seeing the look on my face.. Knowing how you were driving me insane gave you pleasure and just as I begun to come up the stairs you turned and walked into the room looking back over your shoulder begging me to follow you.. As I walk through the door I rip my clothes off my body and tackle you to the bed, tearing the tank top off your body and ripping your boy shorts down to your ankles letting you kick them off.. I let your legs hang and dangle off the edge of the bed as I get down on my knees to bury my face between your legs, licking, kissing and biting your inner thighs.. You begin to drip for me, your legs they start to tremble as that shiver runs down your spine and your back arches just a bit.. Gripping the sheets on either side of you as you whine and rotate your hips into my face while my eager tongue dives deep into your pussy.. As I lift my head up and grip your thighs standing to my feet, I grab your hands and lift you up to stand with me pulling you in close and kissing your lips so that you can taste yourself off me.. Lifting one leg up in my right hand I brace my other on your back as I lay your body down on the bed once more.. Crawling up close to you, lifting your legs in the air and pushing your knees back.. I look in your eyes and pause for a moment as I pull away from you.. You look up at me biting your bottom lip and I feel you slide your hand between your legs to play with yourself, suddenly I grab your body and flip you over onto your stomach.. Lifting your ass in the air bending your knees in towards your body, and with your face buried in the pillows I grabbed your arms and pin them behind your back.. Thrusting myself inside you as I lean harder into your body pushing your face down into the bed even more muffling your screams.. I start to pound your pussy, slapping your ass and making you moan with pure pleasure as you completely surrender to me.. Pinning your arms down into your lower back with one hand I reach down to your head and grab and handful of hair with my other hand and pull your head back towards me.. Your eyes squinting closed biting your lip and screaming out almost in confusion from both the pleasure and the pain.. And as I keep stroking and thrusting myself deeper, harder and faster inside of you I feel you begin to shake, I feel your legs tense up all your muscles flex and even your pussy begin to clench down on my cock.. You explode for me and as you keep cumming I keep fucking, pounding you out as your body trembles and shakes releasing every last drop of cum you have inside you.. Just as you finish with one final stroke I release too, exploding for you and filling you up with every ounce of my cum until finally we both just collapse on the bed and with our last bits of strength hold each other close.. Breathing deeply hearts beating uncontrollably, sweat dripping off our bodies, I can do nothing but kiss your forehead and tighten my hold on you a little more, and then try and figure out where we would get round two, on the bed or on the floor..

§

Thought 6

Not just another ordinary Wednesday, there was something in the air this night.. The way your eyes pierced into my soul as we ate dinner and laughed and talked blissfully as ever.. Every now and then pausing in silence and smiles just awkwardly staring at one another.. As we finished dinner and sipped some wine I cleaned the dishes up while you retreated to the couch to relax and pick out a movie for us to watch.. Quickly finishing my cleanup so I could join you, I lifted your legs up and held your feet in my lap as I sat down.. Still sipping on your wine you start the movie, with no real intentions of watching it.. As I begin to rub your feet and legs, working my way up your calves and to your thighs until my hands begin to wander between them.. Looking over at you I bite my lip as I feel your wetness seeping through your panties from my touch.. Unable to control myself any longer I turn towards you and spread your legs apart positioning myself between them, lifting one leg and bending your knee towards your chest as I lean into to kiss your lips..

Becoming lost in you it feels as though time itself has stopped for a moment as we kiss.. I slide my shorts down around my ankles and lift up your skirt as I slide your panties to the side.. You wrap your arms around my neck and run your fingers through my hair gripping tightly as I thrust myself inside you.. Moaning out for me.. "Papi que Rico, aye dio mios mi amor, give me that dick Joe.." Your words run through my body sending shivers down my spine, I feel as though ice is coursing through my veins.. As I fuck you deeper and harder than you've ever been before I look down into those beautiful eyes, I love to see the pleasure on your face as I look inside your soul.. Biting your bottom lip digging your nails into my chest as I pound that pussy out.. I lean down to whisper in your ear..

"Tell me baby, who's pussy is this.. I want you to tell me who does it belong to.." As I thrust myself a little deeper inside you causing you to scream..

"It's your pussy Joe it's all yours!" As you finish your sentence I kiss you once more attacking your lips and teasing your tongue with mine as I keep fucking you as you continue to moan..

Just when I feel your body get tense as if you're about to cum I stop, pulling out and quickly flipping your body over.. Grabbing your hips and pulling your ass into the air making you arch that back for me, smacking it firmly and gripping it tight.. Teasing your dripping wet pussy from behind with the head of my cock making you beg me for it.. As I reach down and grab your hair to pull your head back towards me I thrust back inside you.. Every inch all at once forcing you to take it all, I feel your body tense up and your pussy clench around my dick.. And you grip the arm rest of the couch and I continuing pulling your head back, smacking your ass until its red and tender giving you an equal amount of pleasure and pain.. I want you to remember this night, remember this feeling and remember exactly how good I made you feel, how good I made you cum.. I feel your body begin to shake and tremble and you start throwing your ass back towards my hips trying to take me in even deeper as your throbbing clit becomes more sensitive by the second and you get closer to the edge.. With one last thrust you scream out..

"Fuck Joe I'm cumming!" And you release for me, exploding and squirting out your cum for me all over my body drenching me in your sweet delicious nectar..

Your legs shaking as I keep stroking until I'm sure you've given me every last drop of cum in your body.. As I pull out and release my grip on your hair your body becomes weak and collapses almost falling off the couch onto the floor.. I scoop you up in my arms and carry you off to the bedroom, laying you down gently as you breathe deeply still trying to calm your heart beat and catch your breath.. A kiss upon your lips as you close your eyes and I pull you in close, wrap my arms around you and whisper softly in your ear.. Telling you how much I adore you, how lucky I feel to be your king, and how lucky I am to have you for my queen.. With one deep breath you sink deeper into me your back against my chest, locking your fingers in mine and pinning my hand against your chest.. And I get lost in the feeling of the rhythm of your heart beat and we both drift off into our dreams..

§

Thought 7

They are beautiful aren't they, the stars in the sky.. The wind blowing off the ocean as the waves crashed down on the shores, I couldn't help but stare at the way the moonlight reflected in your eyes.. It was mesmerizing the way you just captivated all of me, the way you caused this feeling to overtake my body I couldn't resist my urges to take you.. Ravish, is the only word that could come to mind, I wanted to ravish you.. Watching the way your hair blew in the wind, the way you would get shy when I looked at you and smile as you look down and away.. Everything you did was pulling me into you more, attracting me in ways I've never felt before.. I was falling deeper into you and with each passing moment I felt myself beginning to lose control.. I took your hand in mine and pulled your body close to me, looking down into your eyes holding tightly around your waist as I slowly close my eyes and lean in to kiss you.. I feel the breath escape your lips, all the air leaving your body, for a moment you are breathless, frozen somewhere in between space and time as the world around us stops spinning and all that remains are you and I.. Your hands on either side of my face but only barley touching me, trying to process the feeling of floating that has over taken your body.. As I slowly slide my hands down your body, chills over take you at my touch, shivers they run swiftly down your spine.. And as I pull away your eyes remain closed, you take your first breath of fresh air back into your lungs, slowly open your eyes to look up at me and say..

"Joe I want you to take me, right here.. Right now.." As I look down at you somewhere in the middle of disbelief and amazement you bite your lip and run your hands along my chest gripping firmly on my shirt and ripping it completely off my body..

Digging your nails into my bare flesh scratching yourself a trail down to my belt and removing it, followed by my pants.. Reaching your hand into my boxers and wrapping your fingers around my stiff throbbing cock, burying your face in my neck and kissing and sucking on my skin.. That's when I lost it.. Ripping open your blouse letting your full perfectly shaped breasts fall out of your skimpy bra, letting your skirt fall down to your feet as I gently lay your body down.. As the waves crash down on top of us I begin to kiss every inch of you, careful to leave no part of you untouched by my lips.. As I make my way up your chest and to your neck, I slide myself between your legs spreading them apart with my thighs and lifting yours up bending your knees back.. Locking your fingers in mine and pinning them back into the sand above your head, as I slide my throbbing cock gently in and out of your dripping wet pussy giving you just the tip at first driving you crazy.. As you bite my lip and pull me in to kiss you, I thrust myself all the way inside you and you arch your back and let out the sexiest moan I've ever heard.. As you throw your head back taking me all in, every single inch as deep as I can go, I attack your neck and kiss and suck until I leave marks like some kind of animal claiming my territory.. Finding my perfect stroke and rocking your body back and forth to the rhythm of my hips I fuck you until you can take no more, until your eyes begin to roll back and you feel yourself begin to lose all control.. Burying your face in my back and biting down hard as your body starts to shake, your legs tense up and begin to tremble as you get ever so close to the edge.. And then it happens.. With one final stroke you release, letting go and exploding for me in a rush of pleasure and ecstasy.. Screaming out my name as you struggle to arch your back even more thrusting your hips into me as you make sure every last drop of cum makes it way out of your pussy.. As you finish and your body begins to un-tense and relax you sink a little more into the sand, as I lay on top of you breathless and rest my head upon your chest.. The water rushing up around our bodies gently and then retreating back into the ocean.. As you lay there stroking your hands through my hair looking up at the night sky, stars looking down at you.. I feel your arms wrap tightly around my body and hold me close as everything fades to black..

§

Thought 8

5:45pm Thursday evening, we had just left the house and got on the freeway to head out for some drinks and dinner.. On the freeway heading towards downtown immediately stuck in bumper to bumper traffic, rolling the windows up so the dark tint hides us from view of the outside world.. I spark a blunt and turn the music up just a bit, "Wicked Games" playing in the speakers.. I take a few hits and pass it to you and you hit it hard letting the smoke fill you up and begin to elevate your mind and senses.. You sink into your chair a little as you pass it back to me and you feel the music and the high start to take over, the bass bumping through your chest as you close your eyes and begin to grind your hips to the slow deep rhythm of the song.. I take another hit and breath in deep, traffic still not moving, I look over at you and drink you in, suddenly captivated by the way you're working and moving your body in the passenger seat.. As I hand the blunt back to you I reach over and slide my hand between your legs and grip tightly on your inner thigh, you hit the blunt again and lay back in your chair a little letting the seat back down.. The rush that overtakes your body from my touch is over whelming, you reach your hand down placing it over mine as I reach a little deeper between your thighs, slowly running my fingertips along your skin making way towards your pussy.. Rubbing and teasing your throbbing clit through your panties as you begin to drip for me.. Traffic moves just a bit and I turn my head back towards the road and inch up a few feet until coming to gridlock again, keeping my hand between your legs as I do.. Putting the car in park for a moment I turn to you and take both your hands in mine, locking your fingers and pinning your arms above your head around the head rest..

"Don't move baby.." I whisper softly.. As I look you in your eyes and reach my hand back down between your legs..

Reaching over to kiss your lips as you close your eyes and arch your back up in the seat from the feeling of my fingers sliding in and out of your dripping wet pussy.. Gripping tightly on the headrest flexing every muscle in your body as I pull away from you and bite your lip.. Sitting back in the driver seat I turn my attention back towards the road, left hand on the steering wheel, right hand still between your legs.. Just watching the road and driving while teasing you and driving you insane.. You keep grinding your hips and arching your back suddenly every time I touch your most sensitive spots.. Moaning softly but being drowned out by the music pumping through the speakers into the car, the vibrations pulsing through your chest as time seems to slow down and you take in a deep breath.. Feeling your heart start to race in your chest, not sure if it's from the weed or from the euphoric explosion you're experiencing between your legs.. Ac pumping through the vents chilling the cool sweat running down your body and you feel yourself shake and tremble as chills begin to run down your spine.. I feel your thighs and legs start to lock up and your muscles flexing and twitching your body telling me how you were getting closer to the edge.. You reached over to me with one hand and gripped my shoulder so tight digging your nails into my skin through my shirt, the other hand still gripping on the head rest, and I felt you explode.. Letting my fingers slide out and just rubbing on your pussy as you released for me.. Screaming out my name and elevating your voice well above the noise of the music so I could hear you loud and clear, feeling every sensation run through your body as you let every last drop of cum flow out and soak my fingers until I felt you dripping down my forearm.. As you finished I felt you grab my hand from between your legs and raise my fingers up to your mouth to taste yourself off me, careful not to waste a single drop, using your own finger to wipe up some cum that had been dripping down your inner thigh and rubbing it on my lips letting me taste my work.. I began to drool at the taste of you and a craving for your body overtook me in such a way that I could not control myself, in a flash I jerked the steering wheel and turned the car around in traffic to exit off the freeway and head back home.. Looking over at you with a devilish smile I said..

"Fuck dinner I'm taking you home to devour that pussy, I'm sure you won't have a problem with that.." I watched a smile creep its way onto your face as you blew me a kiss and sparked the blunt again sinking back into your seat and closing your eyes blowing smoke into the air and letting yourself drift away as I raced towards home, eager and ready to get my hands on you..

§

Thought 9

You ever just know when you meet someone that you and them would have ridiculously amazing sex.. You just feel this tension, this energy.. Like heat coming off their body it almost makes you sweat a little bit.. Kind of takes your breath away when they speak to you, when everything you envision while trying to keep your composure and speak to them is images in your head of ripping her clothes off and taking her body right there and now.. That moment when you're talking and you both pause and bite your lips realizing you're both imagining what you would do to each other..

I felt this with her..

I felt this feeling when I first laid eyes on her, the first time I heard her voice, the first time I saw her I felt the sexual tension between us thick enough to cut with a knife.. Her eyes.. They entrapped me, it felt as though her stare was creeping deep down into the darkest parts of my soul and she smiled as she read all my secrets.. The way she bit her lips and I watched her look me up and down, I could feel her stripping my clothes off my body and I almost felt the need to cover myself up.. As she looked back up into my eyes I took my turn drinking in her every inch, my eyes roaming her curves and edges slowly disrobing her the same way she did me.. Imagining her jumping in my arms and kissing my lips as she wrapped her legs and arms around me.. I had to reach up and wipe the small beads of sweat beginning to form on my forehead, take in a deep breath and desperately try to find the words to speak to her.. Just as I opened my mouth to speak she raised her finger to my lips to shush me, took my hand and turned away from me pulling me along to follow her.. She lead me through the lobby of the hotel walking just in front of me and I swear I could still feel the warmth and heat radiating off her body.. Her perfect shape in her tight dress as I followed behind examining every inch of her.. Never letting go of my hand she led me into the elevator and pressed the button quickly for the 35th floor, hurrying to close the door so we would be alone, as soon as the doors closed she turned towards me and forced me up against the wall as she held my hands and pinned them down she looked up into my eyes and said..

"Kiss me.." I eagerly obeyed her request and leaned down to kiss her perfect lips, softly and slowly teasing her tongue with mine just a bit as I felt my body overcome with chills from her touch.. I heard the bell ring for the elevator door to open and she pulled away from me taking my hand and leading me out into the hallway and towards her room.. She open the door to her room "3569" .. Lead me inside and closed the door behind us, as she locked it and turned towards me again she simply said "Strip.." I looked at her almost in disbelief, like is this real, could this really be happening, she couldn't possibly be serious.. She noticed me pausing for a second and probably read the confusion on my face as she smile and moved towards me.. Running her hands up my chest and smiling looking up into my eyes she gripped in between the button on my shirt and ripped it off me.. "I said strip.." She said as she slowly backed away from me and walked over towards the bed.. Still slightly in shock but overly excited I began to rip the rest of my clothes off my body and throw them about the room, she let her dress straps down from her shoulder and it fell to the floor around her ankles revealing her naked body, no bra, no panties.. With her back toward me she looked over her shoulder at me and softly said "Take me.."

Walking up behind her and reaching around her body removing her hands from covering her breasts letting her arms fall down to her sides.. As I kiss softly on her neck I tease her breasts and nipples in between my finger tips and reach my other hand down between her legs just barely touching her pussy, teasing her clit just a bit causing her to drip for me and become wet.. As I bite down on her neck and she moans out for me, throwing her hands back and running them through my hair and rubbing her face against the side of mine as I bury myself deeper in her neck kissing and suck viciously.. I quickly spin her body around and pull her in close to me looking down into her eyes for a moment just before I lean down to kiss her lips.. Biting on them slowly as I pull away again and lay her down gently on the bed.. Kissing my way down her neck to her chest, tracing my tongue along her skin out lining every inch of her, making my way down her stomach and stopping just above her pussy kissing her skin softly with my lips.. As I lift her legs up and hang them over my shoulders I dive deep into her burying my face between her thighs and tasting every drop of her wetness.. Flicking her sensitive clit with my tongue teasing her as she began to whine her hips on the bed throwing her hands down and gripping my hair.. As I looked up at her, looking right into her eyes as I continued to kiss and lick between her legs.. She guided my head where she wanted it to go making sure I ate her just right, from all angles touching every spot until I felt her legs begin to shake.. Raising up from between her legs I looked down into her eyes as she laid on her back biting her lips looking up at me, her hands now resting back above her head.. I leaned down towards her and pushed her legs back into her chest bending her knees, placing my hands firmly around her neck and kissing her lips.. I feel her struggling to breathe a little as she moans deeply, I feel her entire body react in shock as she feels me reach between her legs and guide my throbbing cock inside her.. Thrusting in deep giving her every inch and all the breath leaves her body for a moment and as I release her throat and pull away quickly from her lips she screams out.. Pure ecstasy over taking her body and she wraps her arms around my neck digging her nails deep into my flesh causing me to wince a little from the pain.. So I stroke a little harder, a little faster I hit it a little deeper and sweat begins to drip and cover both our bodies.. The smell of sex filling the air in the room her essence intoxicating me as I felt my self losing control becoming completely lost between her thighs..

"Fuck me baby!! Fuck this pussy and make me cum!!" She screamed out loud enough for the people on the floors above and below us to hear her.. Throwing her head and arching her back she thrust her hips into me as I thrust into her and I could feel her body beginning to tremble and shake, her arms releasing from around my neck and slamming down at her sides she began to grip the sheets while moaning and screaming..

I was trying desperately to give her exactly what she wanted, with every stroke I tried going a little deeper, with every thrust I tried going a little harder.. I felt myself becoming addicted to the feeling of pleasuring her, the way she was moaning, the look on her face as she tried to keep her eyes from rolling back in her head just to keep looking up into mine.. It was all so over whelming and she was just so captivating I felt myself completely losing control.. The harder I went the more she kept screaming and begging for more it was like I couldn't give it to her hard enough or deep enough no matter how much I pushed she was begging for more.. Until finally we both could no longer hold back and we finally released.. Both of us together in a pure explosion of ecstasy and erotic euphoria, her cum exploding out of her tight pussy and drenching myself and the sheets and my stiff throbbing cock releasing inside her filling her up with every last drop of cum I had inside my body.. Until we both finished and I collapsed on the bed next to her just falling limp and sinking into the mattress, both of us just covered in sweat and cum, I used the last of my energy to wrap my arms around her naked body and pull her in close to me.. Kissing the back of her neck so softly and just holding her tightly listening to the sound of her heart beat echo inside her chest, the soft rhythm of it just rocked me to sleep as I felt my eyes close and I drifted off into my sweetest dreams..

§

Thought 10

We been arguing and fighting all day, over stupid pointless shit that neither one of us actually care about.. I've reached my limits with this fighting shit, I'm over it and I'm about to put a stop to it.. As I sit on the couch trying to collect my thoughts in a moment of silence while you lay down in the bedroom, angry and pissed at me like no tomorrow.. Maybe I fucked up, maybe you said some dumb shit.. Point is I'm over it and I'm about to get you over it too.. I take one last deep breath, close my eyes and relax myself, upon opening my eyes again I stand up and walk into the bedroom and you turn over and look at me..

Right away you get to bitching.. "Don't even bring your ass in here Joe, get the fuck out I've..."

Before you can even finish your sentence I'm on top of you, pinning your hands back and kissing your lips like you never been kissed before.. In a single moment, with one single kiss I make you forget everything about the last 24 hours and you melt at my touch as if it's the first time all over again.. You let out the deepest sexiest moan I've ever heard in my life and your body instantly relaxes underneath me as you sink into the bed and your legs immediately spread for me.. As I pull away from your lips I bite them and make you flinch a little in between your moaning, lifting your body up so you sit up on the bed and I can rip your shirt off over your head, then laying you back down and tearing your jeans off your legs.. I stand over you for a second and kick off my shorts and boxers, tear my shirt off and throw it across the room.. I crawl back onto the bed and slide myself right between your legs, lifting them up and resting your ankles on my shoulders and bending them back towards your chest.. Looking down at you in those big beautiful eyes of yours I place my hand firmly around your throat and with my other hand I guide my throbbing cock inside your tight, dripping wet pussy.. Just gently at first just giving you the tip, observing the confused look on your face as you begin to forget everything we had been fighting about.. You bite your lip with anticipation as the tip of my cock just slides in and out of you, just teasing your wetness and your sensitive clit.. Just as you begin to move your lips to speak and beg me for this dick I squeeze tight on your throat and thrust myself deep inside you.. Causing you to scream out..

"FUCK JOE!"

Your voice echoes through every room in the house as you moan and scream my name as I stroke you fast and hard pounding that pussy just the way you like it.. Fucking you into an erotic coma forcing you to completely forget ever being mad at me, I feel your body completely surrendering to me.. I keep my grip tight on your throat and wrap my other hand around your right thigh and push your legs further back and thrust even deeper into you..

"Fuck Joe, harder baby, fuck me harder give me all of that dick.."

Your words they pierce me and fill my mind as I close my eyes and get lost for a moment, I have flashes of your words, flashes of how we argued, the yelling and screaming.. Now you're moaning and screaming, it all comes together and I can just feel myself unleash on you.. Fucking you harder than you've ever been fucked, thrusting my hips into you making your body rock to the rhythm of my strokes.. Your hands reaching up and digging your nails into my chest scratching me, I feel the sweat starting to drip on my skin and my body start to tremble.. I see your eyes begin to twitch and try to roll back into your head, your legs beginning to shake and your muscles starting to flex and become tense.. Just as your start to arch your back and scream out I let go of your throat, grab your hands and pin them back behind your head.. Thrusting deep into you one last time and leaning down to kiss your lips we both release and let go.. Exploding for each other as we cum together, your body shaking underneath mine as I keep my hips pressed into you and your back remains arched forcing your hips into me.. Each of us trying to extract every last drop of cum from the other.. And as our bodies shake and convulse a few final times and we both breath again for the first time our bodies become weak and collapse into one another.. I fall beside you and use the last of my strength to pull you in close.. Your back to me and your naked body pressed up against my skin so close you could feel my heart beating on your back.. I wrapped my arms around you and held you tightly, tighter than I've ever held you before, kissing the back of your head and just letting out one last deep breath before slowly fading out and drifting off to sleep.. Not a care in the world and both of us had forgotten what we were ever mad about..

§

Thought 11

The distance between us had kept me from
getting my hands on you for quite some time
now.. Finally the time had come for me to take a
few days off and go visit you, as I sat on the plane
lost in my thoughts of anticipation.. My mind
begun to wander and vivid images started flashing
through my mind, I could almost feel your touch
gently caress my skin and I felt chills run through
my body.. This fucking plane couldn't fly any faster
to get me to you I was absolutely feigning for you,
and finally tonight I would have you.. As I felt the
plane begin to descend and we made our final
approach into the airport, it felt as though time
could not move any slower as I watched the
terminal get closer and closer out my window.. It
was weird, I could almost feel your presence and
my heart beat a little faster as if it sensed you
were near.. Waiting for people to grab their bags
from the overhead compartments and file out of
the plane I sat restlessly tapping my foot wishing I
could somehow just move them all out of my way

and run to you.. Finally as everyone moved out I stood up and made my way off the plane and it felt as though time was slowing down around me but I was moving at a normal pace, I could hear myself breathing and my heart beating in my chest..

You were the very first thing that caught my eyes as I entered the terminal, it was as if I was somehow magnetically drawn to you I felt as though my soul recognized yours.. For a moment everything stopped but you and I, the world ceased to exist along with everyone in it.. The airport disappeared, the shops, the entire world was just gone.. It was as if we were standing in a black hole and all I could do to survive was keep looking in your eyes.. As I reached out to take your hands in mine and pull you close to me, wrapping my arms around your waist and grabbing your ass so tight, looking down into your big beautiful eyes.. I feel you become heavy in my arms as your knees buckle a little and get weak, but only because you feel safe and know that I would never let you fall.. I smile just a bit and you bite your bottom lip and give me that look I can't resist, leaning down towards you I softly kiss your lips, teasing your tongue with mine, suddenly reaching up to grab your face I kiss you deeper than you've ever been before, sending a shock to the core of your soul.. For a moment it feels as though my brain has somehow exploded out of the back of my head, then in a rush I feel everything snap back into me.. As I pull away slowly I bite your bottom lip and stretch it out as you keep your eyes closed, still lost in the fantasy world I've just brought you to.. When I release you from my kiss and you reopen your eyes to look back up into mine we both suddenly feel a rush of uncontrollable desire overtake our bodies and it becomes clear that perhaps we won't be able to wait until we get home.. I grab your hand and quickly turn away pulling you behind me to follow me through the terminal, weaving through the crowds of people and eventually slipping into a back hallway in a darker, less populated section in the concourse.. We slipped into a small storage room they used to keep unclaimed luggage off the baggage claim racks, I quickly slid the door closed behind us and locked it.. Turning back towards you and grabbing you by your waist pulling you in close to me and pushing your back up against the wall, kissing your lips once more and ripping your shirt off your body, reaching down to undo your skirt and let it fall down to your ankles.. I lifted one leg up with my one hand and with the other undid my pants and let them fall to the floor, I felt you reach one hand down and take my throbbing cock into your grip and start to massage and stroke it causing it to grow and stand fully at attention for you.. I bury my face in your neck and begin to suck and bite gently on your flesh causing you to moan out for me and you start begging for me to fuck you..

"Please baby, I've been waiting so long.. Give me that dick Joe.. Give it to me ba…. OH FUCK!" Before you were able to finish begging I lost control.. Thrusting myself up inside you and giving you every inch of me all at once, filling you up and making sure you scream for me..

I continued to stroke and thrust myself deeper and harder inside you touching parts of you that had been yearning for me since the last time you had felt my touch.. I could feel your pussy pulsing for me, clenching down tightly around my cock almost as If you were hugging me to say you missed me so much.. I wanted you to feel like I missed you too.. So I quickly pulled out of you and spun your body around, bending you over and letting you lean forward to grip onto some luggage pieces to brace yourself and without warning I quickly thrust myself back inside you causing you to scream out again..

"Fuck Joe! Make this pussy cum baby, please I'm begging you.." Your screams echoing in the small room and driving me completely insane making me lose all control.. Pounding away at your pussy and pulling your hair making you tilt your head back towards me.. The harder I fucked you the louder you screamed for me and there was nothing that turned me on more than the sound of your voice screaming my fucking name, I had missed it all these months away from you more than you could possibly imagine.. Now it was like music to my ears as I leaned down to bite on your neck some more, tilting your head to the side a little by tightening my grip in your hair.. My other hand grabbing tightly on your waist pulling you closer into me trying to penetrate you deeper than I've ever gone before until I felt your legs begin to tremble and shake, your entire body start to convulse and you started begging me to let you cum..

"Papi!! Please can I cum for you, fuck daddy I want to explode!!" Your begging made me want to release too so I granted you permission..

"Yes my love, cum for me, give me all that delicious cum I want every last drop.." Almost before I could get my sentence out I felt you release..

Screaming out for me in pure ecstasy as you let your juices begin to flow and your sweet nectar drenched my cock and started dripping down both of our legs.. At the same time as your explosion I too had a release, my dick erupting inside of your pulsing pussy and filling you with every last drop of cum in my body.. And when each of us had extracted all the cum from the other I pulled out of you and spun your body back around.. As I fell back against the wall I held you close in a tight embrace and for a moment or two we just stood still, hearts racing and out of breath.. Sweat dripping down each of our naked bodies and as I looked down into your eyes and kissed you once more we both just started smiling and you pulled away biting my bottom lip and stretching it out towards you before whispering softly..

"I missed you so fucking much Joe.. Take me home and give me more of what I been missing daddy.."

§

Thought 12

I was never really a fan of regular, boring, missionary sex.. I mean yeah ok it's cool every now and then if you're just trying to get in a quickie, or its someone you're really just not that into.. I don't know maybe it's just me but it just doesn't do it for me.. I like that wild shit, the kind of sex that makes you question your life after wards as you lay there trying to catch your breath.. The kind of sex that makes you crave more, crave that other person almost like a crack head craves crack.. Sex is powerful, it's passionate, it's not meant to be boring and routine.. You should experiment with that shit, do new things and push the boundaries of your limits with your partner.. This is a story about a girl I once knew, a girl named Susie Q..

Now Susie was no ordinary girl, after a while I started calling her Susie Screw because let me just tell you this woman rocked my world.. Let me tell you about the first time her and I ever met..

Stepping out of my car into the cool evening air it was a little after 6:00pm in the middle of November.. After a long week of work Friday had finally come and the weekend was my time to be free and enjoy life.. Looking up at the big bright illuminated sign on the building that read.. "Crew Lounge and Bar" I stood outside for a moment and sparked up a blunt before going inside.. Feeling the smoke fill my lungs mixed with the cold fresh air my body instantly relaxed and let go of all the weekday stress.. To me there was just no better feeling in the world as I felt myself becoming more lifted by the second.. After about 15 minutes I clipped the blunt and walked inside, taking my jacket off and greeting the hostess as I walked passed and headed straight for the bar.. This being my regular spot most everyone knew who I was and greeted me as I sat down and begun to engage in bullshit small talk with the bartender as she made my drink..

"So Jenny how you been, what's new this week? Oh and I'll take the usual red bull and vodka please."

She replied with some boring ass story about her boyfriend and how he was making her life completely miserable and what not, I just tried to listen and nod my head as much as possible to show interest.. My head was spinning from the high as I listened to her story and sipped my drink trying not to fall asleep.. Then she said something of value, something interesting that caught my attention.. She mentioned seeing a new face in the bar tonight, a woman she's never seen before.. You see I had a bit of a reputation where I was from I was known for three things.. My career, my money, and my women.. Now Jenny said something to me on purpose, that's because she was my wing woman.. I came into this bar every weekend just about when I was in town, it was the nicest spot in the city and besides Jenny and I had been friends since high school she always put in a good word for me with any girl that came to her bar..

"So Joe I seen this new girl tonight, not from around here I think. She's a bit different.." She says to me..

Looking at her and feeling my eyes open up just a bit wider I say to her..

 "What do you mean, different?" Sitting forward and leaning on the bar to listen closely because it's starting to get crowded and hard to hear what she's saying..

"Yeah I don't know she's just different, not the like the girls from around here, she said her name is Susie. I told her all about you, figured you'd be in tonight. She's right over there." And she points over to the corner table under the dim lights next to the water wall.. And then I see her.. My drink dam near slipping out of my hand and falling to the bar..

Just as Jenny was pointing her out and I looked at her she was taking a sip of her drink through the straw delicately holding it with two fingers and looking down as she sucked the liquid up into her perfect lips.. As I remained staring at her frozen and unable to look away she looked up directly into my eyes while she continued to drink and winked at me, almost as if she knew I had been looking.. My jaw dropped and I had to force myself to look away before someone saw me staring at her like that.. I turned back to Jenny and said..

"Holy shit! Who is she, where did she come from, I must have her right now.." I found out as much info as I possibly could from Jenny and finally collected myself and gathered my thoughts together in my spinning head..

This girl was perfect, she was everything.. So unlike any woman I had ever seen in this bar before, so unlike any woman I had ever seen anywhere before.. I had Jenny send the bar back over to her table with another drink of what she ordered the first time and as she got it and he told her who it was from I looked over at her and raised my glass towards her as if to say "cheers".. She did the same and took a drink, then she turned to the people at her table and said something to excuse herself.. She walked towards me and I was trapped, my eyes locked on hers as she got closer everything got quiet, all the people in the bar begun to disappear and go away, the music faded away and everything got quiet.. She walked right up to me and just as I was about to speak and introduce myself she put her finger to my lips and said..

"Shhh, don't speak. Just get up and follow me."

I didn't even hesitate, I had no idea how much my bill was but I didn't care I just threw $200 down for Jenny and got up quickly to follow Susie.. She grabbed my hand and pulled me through the crowd of people who were somehow still non-existent in my eyes, she was all I could see everything else around her was blacked out.. Like she had some kind of spell on me it was incredible.. We finally emerged outside into the cold night air and she turned to face me as she kept walking backwards towards the parking lot.. Then she said..

"Take me home, away from here I want to be alone with you.."

This wasn't real, it couldn't be happening.. I felt as though I might be dreaming but I didn't want to wake up.. I couldn't even speak to her I just nodded my head yes and we walked towards my car.. I opened up the passenger door for her and helped her inside and gently closed the door behind her.. I walked around to my side and quickly got in and started up the car so the heat would start blowing out.. As I revved the engine a little waiting for the car to warm up she suddenly reached her hand over and placed it on my thigh.. She gripped tightly and I looked over at her, watching her eyes go back and forth from mine, to her hand on my thigh, biting her bottom lip and smiling a little.. Without warning she reached over and kissed me, climbing on top of me straddling my legs.. I was almost in shock, I couldn't move and I wasn't sure what to do.. I think she noticed because she reached down and grabbed my hands and placed them on her ass and squeezed them tight forcing me to grip it, then she put her hands in my hair and latched on as she continued to kiss me.. I got the hint and gripped tight on her perfect ass, the harder she pulled my hair the tighter my grip became on her.. The car was nice and warm now and the windows started to fog up and get steamy, I felt sweat starting to drip down my body and she raised up and pulled her shirt over her head, exposing her full perfectly shaped breasts with no bra on.. She wrapped her arms around my head and pushed my face into them making me kiss and suck on her tits and I eagerly obeyed.. Worshiping every inch and teasing her nipples with my tongue making them grow hard and erect.. Kissing my way up to her neck as I reached up and pulled her hair making her tilt her head back and expose that sweet spot to me.. Licking and sucking on it causing her to moan out for me and she started to grind her hips into me as she felt my cock growing through my pants and rubbing against her dripping wet pussy through her panties as she pulled her skirt up.. She grabbed my hair and pulled my head out of her neck and pushed back from me a little, she reached down and unbuckled my belt and ripped my pants open, she raised up a little and I quickly slid them off.. My throbbing cock slipping out and her eyes got big as soon as she saw it, quickly grabbing it in her hands and sliding it into her pussy so slowly as she sat back down.. Straddling my legs once more and taking me all the way inside her, every last inch as she pulled herself close to me and begun to kiss on my neck.. I thrust my hips up into her and she made her hips whine around in circles for me and we matched each other's rhythm and I touched every inch of her.. Forcing myself deep into places that no other man had ever dared to go, fucking her in a way that she could feel it within her soul.. She was overcome with pleasure, pure ecstasy as she reached around me and dug her nails into my back through my shirt, she bit down on my shoulder and I gripped tightly on her hips forcing her down even harder on my dick.. I buried my face in her neck and began to lick and suck her skin, tasting all her pains and regrets of her past in her sweat.. She was giving herself to me in ways she had never thought possible before.. She was screaming, moaning, calling out for me and begging for more..

"FUCK, YES.. Give it to me baby just like that, keep fucking me don't stop.."

Her words pierced through me like a blade, she caused me to completely lose control.. I wrapped my arms around her and gripped her shoulders from the back and pulled her down into me as I thrust a little harder up inside her, increasing the speed of my strokes I started to pound her pussy making her scream.. She sat back a little so I could look in her eyes while I fucked her, biting her bottom lip in between her moaning and screams, I just loved how I could see the way I made her feel written all over her face.. She tried so desperately to keep her eyes locked on mine as she got closer to the edge but the closer she got the more they started to roll back into her head.. I felt her nails dig deep into my skin as she slapped her hands down on my chest and let out one last scream, her legs flexed and squeezed tightly against mine and I thrust up inside her one last time.. She released.. Exploding for me, her cum squirting out soaking my lap and the seat.. I kept stroking in and out of her trying to extract every last drop of cum from her shaking body.. As she kept her head looking down with her eyes closed and hands still pressed firmly into my chest, she kept grinding her hips into me as she came and just as she finished her orgasm she thrust into me one last time and to my surprise I lost control and exploded.. I had been so focused on her cumming I didn't realize how close I was.. My eyes rolled back and my legs shook underneath her as she kept grinding into me and biting her lip as she watched me cum.. I moaned for her and just as I finished and I tried to stay completely still she grabbed my face and kissed me ever so gently as she slowly kept rotating her hips with my cock still inside her and I shook uncontrollably because of how sensitive I was after cumming.. She slowly slid up off of me allowing my cock to slip out of her and my eyes rolled back once more as I sank into the seat and let my head fall back trying to catch my breath.. My heart racing and pounding against my chest as I looked over at her fixing her skirt and putting her shirt back on.. As I reached down and pulled my pants up she looks over at me and says..

"Shall we go back inside for more drinks, or straight home for round two?"

§

Thought 13

I know you like it when I kiss that spot on your neck.. The way your body just melts as my lips touch your skin.. As I gently suck that spot where your shoulder meets your neck, I feel the chills run down your spine and as I pull you in close to me.. You want to hold me back but the way I'm kissing, licking and sucking on that spot is just too much for you to handle.. Your arms fall limp at your sides as you feel your knees get weak and start to shake.. I pick you up and swing your legs around me and you just lock your ankles as I grip tightly on your ass.. Still kissing on your neck, your upper body still weak you just collapse into me as I carry you into the room, all you can do is bite down softly on my shoulder every time I suck a little harder on your neck.. As we get into the room I pull my head away from you and look you deep into your eyes as you bite your bottom lip and look back at me.. I lean in quick and kiss your lips and pull your bottom one stretching it out biting down gently as I slowly pull away and lay your body down on the bed.. Looking down at you I softly say..

"Strip for me baby, take it all off now.."

Before the words can even finish escaping from my lips I see your hands snap up to unbutton your blouse and rip it off your body, unsnapping your bra almost at the same time and throwing them both aside.. Sliding your skirt down slowly around your ankles and I reach down and pull it off for you completely and you just lay back in your black laced boy shorts and bite your lip as you look down at them and then back at me.. Your eyes telling me exactly what you wanted me to do, so I ripped my shirt off and tore my shorts and boxers off and crawled onto the bed.. Beginning to kiss my way up your legs, reaching your inner thighs and biting just a bit as you reached down and locked your fingers in my hair.. As I made my way up I kissed your dripping wet pussy that was soaking through your panties and I bit down on the edge of them and pulled them off you with my teeth.. I slid them down your legs, lifted them up and taking your ankles and resting them on my shoulders.. Grabbing your thighs and sliding your ass down towards me as I bent your knees back I saw your eyes become fixated on my throbbing hard cock between my legs as I leaned in closer to you, just teasing your pussy with the tip rubbing the head back and forth on your sensitive clit.. Moaning out for me you started to beg me for it..

"Joe please give it to me baby, give me that dick, I want...."

Before you could finish I just thrust it inside you, forcing you to take every inch of what you asked for.. Seeing the way your eyes rolled back into your head and all the breath escape your body momentarily.. I almost envy you in that moment because of the pure ecstasy and pleasure written on your face.. You throw your hands down to grip the sheets and pull them up as your muscles flex and tense up.. Your knees bent all the way back touching your chest as I lean into you more forcing myself a little deeper inside you with every stroke.. Pounding out your pussy thrusting into you as hard as I can as I reach down and grab your throat, your body rocking back and forth matching the rhythm of my strokes.. Your moans become screams as my name starts escape from your lips over and over in between random curse words..

"Oh Joe.. Fuck.. Joe yes.. Shit, fuck yes Joe give me that dick babe.."

Your soft voice echoing in my head as I close my eyes and get so lost between your thighs.. Giving you exactly what you're asking me for I love the way your pussy clenches down a little tighter every time I pull out and thrust back inside you.. I feel both of our bodies start to twitch as muscles start to burn and flex the deeper we get lost in this sex, your body starts to shake as I let your legs fall from my shoulders down to the bed.. I lean down into you and bury my face in your neck and begin to suck and kiss your skin, you wrap your arms around me and dig your nails deep into my back as I keep stroking and thrusting my hips into you.. My arms hooked under you gripping your shoulders as I keep attacking your neck I pull you in as close to me as possible trying to fuck you down to your soul.. As you moan and whisper in my ear..

"Ooo daddy just like that Joe, make this pussy cum baby.. Make me cum for you Joe.."

That was when I lost all control.. Gripping even harder on your body and biting down on your neck I thrust inside you as deep as I could go and increased the speed of my strokes and kept pounding you out until I felt you get ready to explode.. I felt your nails dig deep into my skin scratching the fuck out of my back, your legs locked up and started to shake and you stopped breathing and tried to scream out..

"Ffffffuckkkkk... Joe im cumming!!"

And you released.. Body convulsing and every muscle in you flexed up and got tight as your cum came squirting out all over me drenching my body and the sheets in your warm sweet delicious nectar.. As I lifted my head and kissed your lips as I kept stroking in and out of your pussy forcing you to give me every last drop of cum you were holding in your body.. Once you finished and your body finally stopped shaking I released your lips from mine and slowly raised up to look down on you, your eyes still closed, lips still puckered and hands just frozen in the air as if you were still holding the sides of my face.. Covered in sweat and desperately trying to catch your breath I could almost hear your heart beating out your chest.. I collapsed next to you and pulled you in close with your back against my chest, moving your hair to the side and kissing that sweet spot on your neck that started all this and just as I did you turned around to face me and said..

"The fuck you doing?? Get your ass back up, let's go round two.."

§

Thought 14

Nothing like waking up early on a Saturday morning, the sun light peeking through the shades gently kissing my face opening my eyes after a few good hours of rest.. No work today, no calls, no emails, no nothing just an entire day to do anything, such a good feeling as I roll onto my back and cross my arms behind my head.. When you feel me move you begin to stir and wake up, rolling over and throwing your arm across my chest and your leg across mine.. Eyes still closed and you smile as you breath out and whisper..

"Good morning babe, did you sleep good?"

And you softly start to kiss my neck and nibble on my ear and I can feel the chills begin to run through my body.. I try to say good morning back to you but you start to kiss harder and suck on my neck and I find myself moaning for you.. You reach your hand down under the sheets and grab my cock beginning to stroke it softly and slowly feeling it grower harder for you.. I reach my hand down and around your ass as you still lay with your leg wrapped over me, I begin to tease your pussy from behind ever so gently with my fingertips.. You instantly start to drip for me and your hips begin to whine and grind against my body, I feel myself start to shake with anticipation and I can no longer control myself I want to lose control and take you right now.. Just as I try to turn my body to get on top of you I feel you grab both my arms and pin me back down, before I know it your straddling me looking down into my eyes reaching in to kiss my lips.. I close my eyes and feel your lips meet mine and feel a rush of ecstasy overtake me and I just melt under you and no longer resist you holding me down.. As you pull away slowly and bite my bottom lip I keep my eyes closed and I feel you let go of my arms and begin to kiss your way down my body while scratching me with your nails down my chest.. You softly kiss the tip of my dick as you watch it throb and jump for you, looking up at me as you just tease me, licking it as I look down at you and try to control my hips from thrusting up into your mouth.. All I want to do is grab your head pull your hair and shove my dick down your throat forcing you to take every inch, but you made it clear this morning you'll be in control.. So I lock my hands behind my head and continue to watch you tease me as you take my dick in your hand and slowly begin to stroke it and take just the head in your mouth, flicking the tip with your tongue making my eyes roll back into my head.. Then suddenly as you keep stroking you swallow every inch, feeling my dick hit the back of your throat and your lips press against my skin as you gag a little and slide it back out.. Wiping the drool from your mouth you spit on the head of my dick and start jerking it harder and faster.. Gripping my thigh with your other hand and digging your nails into me forcing me to enjoy the mixture of pain and pleasure.. You stop stroking and take my dick in your mouth and suck it while grabbing my balls and looking up into my eyes as I fight them rolling back into my head and try to keep them locked on you.. I reached down and push your hair to the side gently and hold it my hands out of your face, I don't pull it though, just hold it ever so softly as I look down on you and slowly thrust my hips up and down gently fucking your mouth.. You grab my cock tight in your hand just as you felt me twitching as if I was about to cum and you force me to hold it in, looking up at me with a devilish smile and biting your lips as you watch me struggle not to cum.. Kissing your way up my body as you crawl on top of me and straddle me with your legs.. You lean down to kiss my lips and force my hands above my head again and pin them down.. Kissing on my neck and biting my ear I hear you softly start to whisper..

"Do you want this pussy babe, tell me how bad you want it.."

Just before I open my mouth to beg you for that pussy you hold your hand over my mouth and silence me.. Pressing your lips up against your hand on my mouth and looking deep into my eyes I can do nothing but stare back into yours as I feel myself paralyzed beneath you.. You slowly reach down with one hand and take my throbbing hard dick in your grasp as you raise your hips up a little and tease your dripping pussy with the head a bit.. I try thrusting my hips up inside you and every time I do you pull away just out of reach, driving me fucking insane as I moan for you.. Just when I feel like I've had all I can take and you feel my body becoming restless under you I feel you slide down on my cock taking in every inch of me all at once.. Beginning to grind your hips into me and ride my dick as you slap your hands down on my chest and dig your nails into my flesh.. I reach my hands down and grip tightly on your hips and just hold on for the ride.. You thrust your hips back and forth into me taking my dick inside you as deep as I can possibly go, looking down into my eyes as you bite your lip and moan for me telling me how good it feels to have me inside of you.. Leaning in to kiss my lips and tease my tongue with yours, your chest pressed against mine and your hips still continue to whine.. I thrust my hips up into you every time you thrust yours down into me, trying to penetrate that pussy deep enough to fuck your soul.. The deeper I go the more you dig your nails into my chest and the tighter I grip on your hips and ass.. As you slowly pull away from my lips and stretch my bottom one out biting on it softly I feel your legs tense up and start to shake.. I wrap my arms around your body and pull you in as close to me as possible making you bury your face in my neck and you begin to kiss and suck on my sweet spot as you keep bouncing up and down on my dick.. As I feel your body start to shake even more I feel my own legs tense up and my muscles all flex letting me know I was getting closer to the edge.. I released my arms from being wrapped around you and you push yourself up and throw your hands down on my chest again, throwing your head back and screaming out telling me you are about to cum.. I feel your nails dig in just a little deeper and everything freezes for a moment as I feel your pussy clench down on my cock one last time before you thrust into me and release, drenching my body in your cum, soaking the sheets.. And at the very same time I thrust my hips up into you, and I explode.. Releasing all my cum for you and filling you up being sure to give you every last drop stored in my body.. Both of us shaking and screaming as we cum together and finally you collapse on top of me as we both finish.. Breathing heavy and your head resting on my chest you feel my heart racing and I feel yours pounding, desperately trying to catch our breath.. As you look up at me and smile, kissing my chest and biting me softly you look up me to say..

"That was amazing babe, now how about breakfast in bed.."

§

Thought 15

From the tone of your voice I can tell you just didn't have a good day, I sense that today was just one of those days where everything went wrong and you just couldn't get right.. As you sit across from me at the table and tell me stories of your day I just can't help but get lost in your eyes, the way the light reflects in them is mesmerizing.. I'm addicted to you in such a way that I hang on every word you speak with anticipation of the next to escape your lips, the sound of your voice is even enough to get my heart racing a little faster.. The more you speak and look into my eyes the more I feel myself giving in to you, becoming lost in you without you even trying.. Innocently speaking to me and fully unaware of what you are doing, ignorant to the fact that in this very moment I want to jump across the table and kiss you deeply just before I strip your clothes off and ravish your perfect body.. My eyes must be wandering because all of a sudden you stop speaking and as the silence hits me my eyes snap back up to yours and I notice you tilt your head a little looking at me rather curiously..

"Is there something on your mind babe.."

You ask me as you slowly stand up and walk over to me, throwing your leg over me and straddling my lap.. I can't even answer as I just stare at your perfect breasts poking out of your blouse in my face, I just bite my lips and nod my head yes..

"Well baby why don't you tell me what's on your mind, better yet I know how to get it out of you.."

Just as you finish your sentence you grab my face and kiss my lips so deeply and so passionately it feels as though a surge of electricity pulses through my body.. I can't fully describe to you the feeling I felt because never had I felt such a feeling before.. As you teased my tongue with yours and slowly pulled away biting my lip and stretching it out as you open your eyes once more to look at me.. I seem dazed, lost in another world somewhere far away from here, my eyes still closed and my heart pounding against my chest as

I still feel you on my lips.. You smile and stand up grabbing my hand and pulling me up to follow you into the bedroom..

You spin me around and push me down onto the bed telling me to take my shirt off over my head as you undo my belt and rip my pants off my legs, standing over me and examining my body as you slowly start to strip for me.. As I watch you undo every button of your shirt and slide it off and then your tight skirt rolling down your legs and off your body, my cock begins to grow for you and you notice as I see your eyes become fixated and you bite your lips in anticipation.. Undoing your bra strap and exposing your full perfectly shaped breasts and your erect nipples, then sliding your panties down around your ankles and kicking them off I begin to twitch on the bed and as I sit up to get my hands on you, suddenly you lift your leg and put your foot on my chest.. Pushing me back down and climbing on top of me, grabbing my arms and pinning them down above my head, looking down on me with those big beautiful eyes staring right into my soul.. Leaning down to kiss my lips once more and making your way down to my neck burying your face into me and kissing and sucking on my skin.. Your legs straddling me I started to feel you grind your hips into me, whining them so slowly up against me and I felt your dripping wet pussy brush up against my throbbing cock.. I started to become restless underneath you, thrusting my hips up into you as I moaned a little every time you bit down softly on my neck.. You whispered softly in my ear..

"Tell me papi, do you want this pussy, tell me how bad you want me.."

Nibbling on my ear as your words pierced right through me as if you were speaking directly to my soul.. I moaned for you as I continued trying to thrust myself inside you every time you rubbed your wetness against me..

"Baby please I need that pussy, give it to me now, I'm begging you.."

Just as I finished my sentence you kissed my cheek and sat up by pressing your nails into my chest, lifting your ass up just a bit and reaching down with one hand taking my throbbing hard cock and guiding it so that just the tip slid up inside you.. Reaching down again and planting both hands firmly on my chest you look down into my eyes as you slowly slide down on my cock and raise back up over and over taking every inch one at a time as you bite your lips never breaking your gaze into my soul.. When I could take no more of this tease and torture I threw my hands forward and grabbed tightly on your ass and pushed you down while I thrust my hips up onto you.. Forcing you to take me in all the way filling you up with every inch as deep as I could reach..

"Aye dio mios papi.. Oooh fuck Joe.."

As you scream out I felt myself losing all control and the wild beast within me began to unleash itself, my hips uncontrollably thrusting up into you trying desperately to fuck you in a way you've never known before.. I wanted to make you fucking scream my name until you lost your voice and you released your cum for me.. My throbbing cock forcing its way in and out of your tight dripping pussy and I could feel you clenching down around me tightly.. I felt your legs start to tighten up and flex around me straddling my waist even tighter and all your muscles starting to flex as your body was telling me how close you had gotten to the edge.. So with one final thrust I made you release for me, exploding and giving me every last drop of cum stored up in your body and drenching me in your delicious nectar.. My body dripping with sweat and your cum, the sheets stained and saturated as you continued to ride my cock and dig your nails into my chest until you finally finished cumming and just collapsed on top of me.. Your heart beating so hard inside your chest I felt it pounding against mine, completely out of breath and weak I just wrapped my arms around you, held you close and tight and let you drift off into your dreams to meet you for round two..

§

Thought 16

I had noticed you, sitting across the coffee shop from me typing away on your laptop, hair tied, glasses on, make up off.. Baggy t-shirt kind of hanging off your left shoulder a bit revealing your purple bra strap.. Skin tight jeans on showing off your every curve with some brand new Retro's on your feet.. Some people would look at you and say plain.. I looked at you and saw natural perfection, it was so obvious how comfortable you were with yourself and your body and it immediately captured my attention.. I sat back in my chair just gazing over at you until you had no choice but to feel me and look up.. Just winking at me and smiling as you looked back down at your screen again, I sat there just puzzled by you.. Such radiance, such effortless beauty I couldn't help but become lustful, and to top it all off you begun to play along and tease me.. Running your fingers slowly along your thighs sliding your fingers between your legs as you looked back up at me locking your eyes in mine and biting your bottom lip.. I almost found it hard to believe I was awake and not dreaming as I stared back at you frozen and trapped in your eyes, watching you as you continued to tease yourself between your legs.. After what seemed like an eternity you finally reached up and closed your laptop and begun to gather your things, stopping briefly to scribble something on a piece of paper before standing up to walk towards me.. Just as you walk past my table you drop the note down and wink at me as you keep it moving and walk right on by.. I didn't pick up the note immediately because I just couldn't stop staring at you as you walked away and disappeared from my sight.. Then I turned back and just stared at it for a moment, almost nervous to pick it up and read it.. I finally did and my hands shaking I unfolded it to read what was written.. In cute little bubbly handwriting read your name and number with a short message under that read "My Place in 20" and under that was your address.. I must be dreaming, this couldn't be real, but at this point I didn't care if it was a dream or not.. I quickly scooped up all my shit and rushed out to my car and raced to the address you had written down..

I arrived approximately 17 minutes later and parked in the street just in the front of the house, shutting off my car and just sitting there for a minute or two to collect my thoughts.. This was kind of crazy, was I really about to go in this house and meet this stranger I just saw in a coffee shop, I mean you are fine but this is crazy right??

My very next thought was of how fine you looked and how you were teasing me in that coffee shop, the way our eyes locked and we connected..

"Fuck it.." I said to myself..

I'm going in this house and I'm going to make you mine, I'll never forgive myself if I don't, what if I never see you again.. So I take the keys from the ignition and open the door and walk up to the house, just as I'm about to reach for the doorbell and ring it you open it and my jaw hits the floor..

"What took you so long boy.." You say as you stand there with on hand on your hip wearing nothing but some heels, and some black laced panties with no bra, just the smallest little tank top I've ever seen in my life..

I'm frozen, speechless and just looking you up and down drinking in every inch of you with my eyes.. Seeing that I was clearly paralyzed you just roll your eyes and take my hand to pull me inside.. Closing the door behind us and leading me silently up the stairs behind you as my eyes are just fixated on your perfect ass right in my face switching back and forth every time you walk up a step.. We enter into your bedroom and instantly the smell of the burning candles hits me and the aroma of sexual passion and desire overtake my senses.. I become intoxicated by your energy you've created in your little sanctuary, I feel as though you've just granted me access into some kind of forbidden place that no man has ever seen before.. You walked me over to the edge of the bed and sat me down standing in between my legs and spreading them apart with yours, wrapping your arms around my neck and looking down into my eyes for a brief moment before leaning down to kiss my lips.. Feels like my brain is blown out the back of my head, all my breath leaves my body and I am instantly taken away from here, everything fades away but you and I and it's as though we've become surrounded by white clouds as we float somewhere off in wonderland.. You slowly release me from your kiss and as you pull away biting my bottom lip and stretching it out ever so gently before letting it snap back to my face.. I try to breath but find it hard, try to open my eyes but I am gone.. Lost in this place you've brought me to still floating on the clouds, finally I'm able to blink my eyes open to reveal you standing before me once more.. You smile a bit with a devilish grin as you stand over me and begin to strip what little clothes you have on, kicking off your heels as you pull my hands to stand me up and lift my shirt over my head and undo my belt letting my pants fall to the floor.. Never letting my eyes unlock with yours you lean in towards me and I tilt my head down to kiss your lips once more as I feel your hands wander down my body and reach into my briefs.. Rubbing and massaging my throbbing hard cock feeling it grow for you in your hands.. I feel my knees get a little weak and buckle from your touch and I feel you release your lips from me and push me back onto what used to be the bed but is now a fluffy white cloud.. I gracefully float down in what seems like slow motion and just sink into the soft cushion as I feel you rip my boxers off me and throw them aside.. You kneel down before me and I look down at you as you look up into my eyes and begin to run your nails along my skin.. Scratching from my knees up my thighs and onto my stomach just above my throbbing cock as you lick your lips in anticipation of tasting me.. Taking me in your hand and slowly starting to jerk as you just flick the tip with your eager tongue watching as I struggle not to let my eyes rollback into my head.. Never breaking your gaze looking up at me and as you smile again and wink at me you instantly swallow me whole, taking every inch and pressing your lips up against my skin as you try to choose between breathing and choking.. Jerking my cock off at the same time as you swallow me and allow the tip of my dick to touch the back of your throat, pressing your lips up against my pelvis.. I slowly reach my hands down and grip your head and wrap your hair in my fingers, pulling gently and guiding your head up and down and thrusting my hips into you fucking your face.. Looking up into my eyes and winking at me as I bite down and lick my lips wishing I could taste you too, and as if you were inside my thoughts and heard me you swing your legs around to straddle my face, never taking my cock out of your mouth and lowering your pussy onto my very eager and waiting tongue.. We begin to pleasure each other simultaneously and both of us moaning and trying desperately to make the other cum.. My tongue flicking back forth and teasing your sensitive clit while your tongue was working magic of its own on the tip of my cock.. I could feel my eyes rolling back in my head and my toes beginning to curl.. I felt you dig your nails into my thighs as your legs flexed around my face and I felt your grip tighten straddling my face.. At the same time I felt my cock start pulsing and throbbing uncontrollably inside your mouth and my legs also began to tremble and shake.. Both of us just moments away from releasing and exploding and with one final lick and flick from each of our tongues it happened, you cumming first and moments later I follow your lead and let go and lose control.. Both of us trembling and shaking as we keep licking and sucking trying to extract every last drop of cum from the other as greedily as we could possibly devour one another, so careful not to waste a single drop.. Just as you finished sucking the cum from my cock you popped me out of your mouth and turned to look down at me over your shoulder as I was still eagerly licking away trying to clean up the mess you just made, you look down on me to say..

"Such a good boy you are, now it's time for you to really please me.." I feel you wrap your hands tightly around my cock and grip my throbbing shaft.. Your eyes piercing into me and overwhelmed with excitement and pleasure when suddenly I felt the room starting to spin and I faded off.. As I opened my eyes and snapped back into reality I find myself back in the coffee shop staring down at the note you had left me on the table.. It was all a dream, none of it had actually happened.. Yet..

§

Thought 17

Tonight is one of those nights where I feel the need to take control, a little more than usual.. I have plans for you this night my love, many plans for you indeed.. I intend to remind you who that body belongs to, who the true master of your pleasure really is.. Surely you have not forgotten since the last time we played my little game, I remember quite well the way I made you beg and scream my name.. Look at you now down on your knees, a goddess yes, but tonight you are here to serve.. Tonight you will have pleasure but understand this my Queen you must also experience just a bit of pain.. Your submission is required on this cold winter night and I've lit the fire place so as to keep your naked body warm after I've commanded you to strip and take your place down on your knees.. As I stand before you looking down into those big beautiful eyes as you bite your lip looking back up at me, stroking my hands through your hair softly at first, when suddenly I grip tightly and pull your head back..

You wince for a moment feeling your first rush of momentary pain for the evening and chills run instantly through your body, your eyes immediately snapping back open to become locked in our gaze once more.. For the first time the silence is broken by my words..

"My love are you ready to please me..?" Gripping a little tighter on your hair letting you know I require a response..

"Yes Papi.." You softly utter out still looking up into my eyes as you see a smile start to form in the corners of my mouth..

With my left hand I reach into my briefs and pull out my throbbing cock that you've been drooling in anticipation for this entire time.. Your eyes light up with pure joy as I hold it just out of reach from your waiting lips, as I keep my grip on your hair preventing you from swallowing me whole as you so desperately desire to, I speak to you again..

"Tell me my love, would you like to make me happy.." I ask..

"Yes, Papi I'll do anything to please you.." You quickly reply..

I just can't help but smile with joy as you struggle to look away from my eyes but your gaze keeps being drawn to my pulsing cock just out of your reach..

"I want you to beg me for it, beg me for this cock.." As I tilt your head back forcing you to look into my eyes.. You eagerly begin to beg..

"Please Papi! Please give me that cock please give it to me I'll do...."

Before you can even finish I decided that you begged good enough and I forced myself inside your mouth pushing apart your opening lips before you said another word.. Your hands immediately swinging from behind your back to around my waist as your head begins to move in sync with the rhythm of my hips and I slowly begin to force you to take every inch of me.. Your lips pressing up against my skin as I felt myself pulsing inside your mouth touching the back of your throat.. You having to choose between choking and gaging, or moaning and breathing, and at this point your undeniable skills causing my knees to shake and tremble a bit feeling as though they might buckle beneath me.. Fearing that you might make me cum I pull out of your mouth and allow you to sit back on your knees once more to catch your breath.. Then taking your arms I bring you to your feet and walk you over to the bed, telling you to lay down on your stomach, of course you eagerly obey..

Spreading your legs apart and strapping your ankles in the restraints attached to the bed posts, and locking your arms behind your back with wrist straps, I have you right where I want you.. With your face down in the bed your moans of anticipation are muffled by the sheets and your pussy just drips for me as I slowly run my fingertips down your back and when my hand reaches your ass I firmly plant my hand and grip tightly..

"SMACK!"

"Now my love are you ready for the real fun.." I ask, as you feel me crawl up on the bed behind you and wrap my hands around your thighs gripping tightly jerking them back towards me forcing your ass up in the air even more and your back to arch for me..

I gently begin to tease your dripping pussy with just the tip of my cock, swirling it slowly in circles just to stimulate your throbbing clit causing you to moan for me.. You begin to beg..

"Please Papi, give it to me, give me that.." Once again your words are cut short..

Suddenly you feel me thrust myself inside you, forcing you to take every inch all at once as deep as I can possibly go.. I reach down and grab your wrists still tied behind your back and I pull your arms back towards me forcing your head to lift up off the bed and you scream out..

"Fuck Joe!!!" My name escaping from your lips as if it had been trapped inside you for a lifetime..

With my other hand I gripped your thigh and forced your body into me as I continued to thrust my hips into you, fucking you deep enough to reach into the darkest forgotten parts of your soul.. Your moans and screams they cheer me on and force me to become so lost and out of control as I find myself almost blacking out with the pleasure of taking your body in a way that no man has ever dared to before..

I can feel you starting to shake, your entire body beginning to tremble as I see your toes start to curl locked in your restraints.. I pull your arms back even more and reach up to grab your hair with my other hand to tilt your head back almost making you look at me.. Your biting your lip and your eyes rolling back as I keep pounding away at your pussy and with every stroke I feel you grow more tense and you clench down tighter on my cock as I force myself a little deeper inside you.. Just when I feel your about to cum I speak to you again..

"Beg me to cum, beg me for it right now.." As I pull your hair a little harder..

"Please Joe, please let me cum, fuck please.." You manage to utter that sentence out between your moans and screams..

"You may cum for me my dear, give me every last drop.." I barley have enough time to give you permission before I feel you release..

"OH FUCK JOE! Im cumming!!"

And you explode as I thrust into you with one final stroke.. I feel your legs shaking and your body convulsing as you cum for me and give me every last drop you've got inside of you.. Feeling your warm sweet nectar drench my body as you squirt for me and make a mess of the sheets.. Screaming out my name and various profanities proclaiming the absolute pleasure and ecstasy that overtakes you as your orgasm completes.. Finally finishing when I've extracted the last of your cum I release your wrists from their restraints and your legs as well and allow you to collapse onto the bed.. Heart racing, sweat dripping down your body and completely out of breath, myself the same.. I collapse next to you and use the last of my energy to wrap my arms around you and pull you in close whispering in your ear..

"Ok your turn.."

§

Thought 18

Blowing smoke into the air and through the fading cloud your silhouette dances slowly, drenched in the moonlight peeking through the open window as you whine your hips and run your fingertips slowly along your skin.. Arousing yourself just for me as I sit back and burn this loud and get high off you, my free hand gripping tightly on the arm rest of the chair trying desperately to control myself from attacking you and throwing you down on the bed across the room.. Twitching in the chair just drinking in every inch of you with my eyes, your perfect body and every curve, your beautiful face, and those eyes..

When I looked into your eyes I found myself lost in a place I had never known before, a place that does not exist to the mortal eye.. You were a Goddess, worthy of my worship and tonight I intend to do just that, I intend to make your body my temple and my offering to you will be my own..

As I inhale another hit I feel the smoke fill my lungs and hit me hard, chills run through my body as though I have ice in my veins and I close my eyes for a moment to maintain my composure.. You notice the high starting to kick in for me and step closer towards the chair where I am sitting, I feel you take the blunt from my hand and straddle my lap.. I open my eyes and just look up into yours, you throw one arm around my shoulder and hit the blunt in your other hand.. Throwing your head back and blowing smoke up into the air and that was about when I lost control.. Wrapping my arms around you and burying my face into your neck as I pulled you close to me.. Kissing and biting softly on your skin and causing you to moan for me and start to slowly grind your hips into mine.. I reach my hand around and grab hold of your hair and pull your head back a little making my way down your neck to your chest, kissing and sucking on each of your perfectly shaped breasts.. Flicking your nipples just a bit with my tongue and causing them to become erect, still pulling your head back as you reach your hand up and take another hit from the blunt.. Blowing out your smoke and letting the high hit you just as hard as me, that feeling of pure euphoria and ecstasy taking complete control of you.. Just as you were taking one more hit before you blew it out I pulled you in close suddenly to kiss your lips and just as we locked together you exhaled allowing the smoke to go from your lungs to mine, a kiss for our souls is what it felt like.. Just as we released from our kiss you wrapped your arms around me tightly and pressed your face up against mine to whisper softly in my ear..

"Take me, take me right now Joe.. Do you want me Papi?"

Your words sent shivers down my spine, I didn't even feel the need to answer you with a response, I just gripped your waist and stood up from the chair with you in my arms and carried you over to the bed.. I felt your arms wrap tightly around me and your nails dig into my back as your started biting on my shoulders and neck.. You bit down hard one last time before I tossed you on the bed and for a moment just looked down at your naked body, your hands teasing yourself running along your skin making way to in between your legs.. I quickly ripped off my shirt and shorts and revealed my stiff throbbing cock to you, watching your eyes become instantly fixated on it and you bite your lips.. Grabbing your ankles I pulled you down closer to the edge of the bed and forced your legs back towards your chest and bent your knees, climbing on the bed and positioning myself between your thighs.. Looking down into your eyes never breaking our gaze for a moment, you still biting on your lip and whining your hips underneath me trying to get your dripping wet pussy to rub against my pulsing cock.. With one hand I reach down and grip your throat just a bit and make it just a little hard for you to breath, my other hand reaching down and slowly starting to tease your pussy with just the tip of my cock.. I saw your eyes beginning to twitch a little in your head trying to roll back from the feeling of pure pleasure and just as you were about to open your mouth to beg me for it I thrust myself inside you all at once, forcing you to take every inch as deep as I could go..

"OH FUCK JOE!"

You scream out and instantly arch your back and throw your head back, your hands slam down on the bed and you grip the sheets so tight your knuckles become white.. Moaning and screaming a little louder with every stroke I take as I try desperately to go deeper with every thrust of my hips.. Aiming to please your mind, body, and soul.. Looking down at you and watching you struggle to look back into my eyes because every time I thrust inside you it causes your eyes to close and roll back.. Biting my lip and increasing my intensity a little more I feel myself starting to lose control becoming completely lost in you, completely in a trance and my only purpose in life is your pleasure.. Gripping a little tighter on your throat with one hand and the other wrapped around your right leg I push my hips into you a little more and bend you almost completely in half and your ankles cross around my head and neck.. I begin to pound your pussy out and make you scream my name repeatedly as if it is the only word you know in the entire English language.. I feel your body growing more tense with every stroke, your legs begin to shake and all your muscles begin to tighten up and flex..

"Fuck Joe! Papi I'm gonna fuckin cum!"

You scream out and your words echo in my head and I really lose control, thrusting into you a few final times harder and deeper than I had gone all night causing you to release and let go.. And you explode.. Cumming so hard and squirting out so much of your sweet nectar it almost forces my cock to burst out of you, all your juices escaping your body in a rush and I keep thrusting into you trying to extract every last drop as you shake and convulse underneath me and just as you finish I pull out with one last stroke and explode myself, releasing my cum all over your dripping wet pussy and stomach as you just lay there and play with your extra sensitive clit feeling me climax for you.. When I finish I fall forward onto my arms and look down into your eyes, both of us covered in sweat and cum and desperately trying to catch our breath.. I just can't help but lean down to kiss your lips and as I pull away slowly you bite my lip and stretch it out, as I breath out and smile with my eyes closed I whisper..

"So round two in the shower?"

§

Thought 19

"Tell me baby, have you been a good girl today.."

My words reach out and touch you as they echo through your mind, and you feel my breath on your neck as I whisper in your ear.. Sweat dripping down your naked body as you find yourself on your knees in the middle of the bed, blindfolded and your arms restrained above your head to the ropes hanging from the four corner posts.. The gag in your mouth makes it a little hard for you reply to me, drool beginning to drip down your breasts, as you nod your head from side to side as if to say no..

"You haven't been a good girl baby, oh no well that's not good my love.." As a smile creeps onto my face suddenly pain overtakes your body and a loud slap echoes through the room and you feel my hand plant firmly on your ass.. "If you haven't been a good girl for me that means you're a bad girl, and bad girls get punished baby.."

You feel a rush of pleasure and anticipation as my words caress your body while my fingers trace your outlines.. Filling you up with heightened sensations of my touch as you struggle in your restraints and blindfold, moaning through the gag still shoved in your mouth.. As I climb on the bed and kneel behind you, biting softly on your neck while I reach my hands around your body and pinch your nipples in between my fingertips ever so gently.. The way you moan through that gag and struggle in your restraints is so fucking sexy its driving me insane.. As I pull your body close to mine you can feel my throbbing cock brushing up against you from behind as I slide it up under you just barely teasing your dripping wet pussy..

"Do you want it.. Do you want Daddy to fuck that pussy.." Whispering softly in your ear.. As your throw your head back and moan even louder for me..

Grinding your hips up and down trying to find the tip of my swollen cock.. I grab your hair and push your head and body forward, spreading your legs apart more and forcing you to arch your back and stick your ass up in the air for me.. Your arms pulled back and up by your restraints your upper body just hangs in the air suspended off the bed..

My hand still gripping on your hair I pull your head back and I begin to tease your pussy with the head of my cock sliding it in only just a bit.. Just letting the tip drive you insane as I feel your pussy throb and try to clench down and pull me all the way inside you.. You begin to try and scream through your gag, trying desperately to beg for this dick, I could feel you trying to force your hips back towards me doing everything you possibly could to take me inside you..

"SMACK!"

You scream with pain as you feel my hand come down on your ass instantly turning you red and I squeeze tightly gripping on it letting you know exactly who the fuck you belong to.. Before you have a chance to recover from the sting of my slap I thrust forward and force myself deep inside you all at once giving you every inch without warning.. I can hear you trying to scream through your gag but your words are trapped inside of you and all you can do is enjoy the over load of pleasure you are experiencing.. Stroking back and forth my hips slapping hard against your flesh as I pound that pussy and pull your hair nice and tight, and with my other hand repeatedly slapping that ass making sure to give you just the right mixture of pain and pleasure.. I see your hands grab tightly on your restraints still pulling your arms back behind you and suspending your body off the bed, you grip tightly and pull harder on them as your body tenses up and your muscles tighten and flex.. Your legs begin to shake and tremble with every stroke I take.. My stiff throbbing cock thrusting deep inside that pussy, touching parts of you I've never known before..

Your bare ass completely red and covered with my hand marks from the continued slapping, you don't know at this point whether your moaning or sobbing as the drool continues to drip from your gag.. Your moaning drives me crazy and forces me to lose control.. I pull your head back even harder as I tighten my grip, I feel my ab muscles flex and my thighs start to shake.. My body letting me know I'm getting close to the edge and I'm about to cum, and just as I take one last stroke and I release I pull out of your pussy and I explode.. Drenching your body in my warm thick cum, you can feel it pouring out of my cock and covering your ass and back.. As you moan in agony feeling your jealous pussy throb and tingle between your legs.. As my body jerks and shakes and I feel the last few drops of cum release onto you, and I look down upon you and admire my work, the way you look suspended there with your hands pulled back behind you, on your knees with your pussy still dripping between your legs.. Your blindfold and gag both still securely fastened, completely dominated and used just like a bad girl deserves to be treated.. But I'm feeling a little generous after my amazing orgasm so perhaps I'll be a little kind to you.. You feel me release one of your hands from its restraint and let it fall down to your side, you wait for me to release the other by after a few moments you don't feel anything happen.. Hearing my footsteps getting further away you hear me say..

"There you go, finish yourself off, you have until I get back to make yourself cum.." And you hear the door slam shut behind me..

§

Thought 20

After such a long day there's only two things I
want to do.. The first is roll a blunt and smoke the
day away, the second is to strip you down and
ravish your body, taking all my frustrations out on
you.. Feeling the smoke fill my lungs as I take my
first inhale and feel my body start to tingle, my
eyes kind of roll back as I blow smoke out into the
room.. As I sit there and smoke I just watch you
lay on the bed, walking over to you I let you take a
few hits and you feel the THC course through your
entire body.. Blowing out smoke and through the
cloud as it dissipates your eyes fall on me,
suddenly you feel overcome with lust for me and
you begin to crave my body.. As I take my last few
hits of the blunt and put it out I turn back towards
you to see you stripping of your clothes ever so
slowly.. Sliding your shorts down your legs and
kicking them off towards me.. Lifting your tiny
tank top off over your head and just lying there in
your panties and no bra.. Looking up at me as you
lick your fingers and begin to tease your nipples in

between them I see them grow and become erect.. I lick my lips in anticipation of worshipping your body, I rip my clothes off and jump on the bed positioning myself on top of you.. Grabbing your arms and pinning them above your head and holding you down as you struggle a little underneath me.. Looking down into your pretty eyes not speaking a word, just drinking you all in and thinking of all the things I want to do to you.. I watch you as you bite your lip and your eyes roam down my body and become fixated on my throbbing hard cock dangling between my legs just inches away from your dripping wet pussy.. As your eyes snap back up and look Into mine I can't help but lose control and kiss your lips, attacking them with mine and teasing your tongue with mine.. The moment our lips touch I feel your heart begins to beat faster, you begin to softly moan for me as you start to whine your hips beneath me and try to thrust yourself up into my cock.. I press my hips up against yours and force myself down on you, pressing my cock up against your wetness through your panties, hearing you moan a little louder as I do this.. I begin to kiss my way from your lips to your neck, sucking and biting just a bit as I let go of your arms and you wrap them around me gently caressing my back and running your fingers through my hair.. I make my way with my lips from your neck down to your breasts, kissing and worshipping them taking each nipple in my mouth and flicking them with my tongue driving you absolutely insane.. You begin to speak between your moans..

"Aye dio mios papi, fuck me Joe please give me that dick I can't take it no more.."

Smiling with delight and excitement as I listen to you beg and continue to kiss and tease your body, working my way from your breasts, licking my way down your stomach till I reach just above your pussy.. Playing with the waist band of your panties just teasing you a bit more with my fingertips, I suddenly rip them off of you and expose that pretty pussy to me.. Already soaking and dripping on your inner thighs I immediately begin to kiss and lick around it careful not waste a single drop of you.. Your moans grow louder the closer my tongue gets to your pussy and as I look up at you and smile I just flick your clit with my tongue causing your entire body to twitch as I drive you crazy.. I plunge my tongue deep inside you burying my face between your thighs as I proceed to lick and suck your pussy as you reach your hands down and grip my hair, guiding my head between your legs making sure I eat you from all the right angles just the way you like it.. Sliding my shoulders underneath your legs and wrapping my arms around them gripping tightly on your thighs pulling you in closer to me, burying my face between your legs as deep as I can possibly go.. When I feel your muscles start to flex and get tense I immediately stop tasting you and raise my head up to look into your eyes once more, you look down at me with a mixture of pleasure and confusion on your face and I can see you trying to figure out why I stopped when you were so close to cumming.. I slowly kiss my way up your body and trace your outlines with my tongue all the way up to your neck and I bite you softly and then kiss your lips letting you taste yourself off mine.. You can't help but moan for me as my tongue teases yours and I reach my hand down between our legs and begin to tease your pussy with the tip of my cock, just rubbing it against your sensitive throbbing clit.. Just as you open your mouth to beg me for it cut you off quickly and thrust myself inside you, forcing every inch as deep as I can possibly go.. Your head snaps back and your eyes roll back inside your head as you throw your arms around me and dig your nails into my back.. As I stroke my hips back and forth and pound your pussy out making you scream for me..

"Aye papi que Rico, fuck me hard Joe.. Make this pussy cum baby.."

Eager and happy to oblige your requests I increase the speed of my stokes and raise up to look down on you, bending your knees back to touch your chest and placing one hand around your throat firmly.. As I look deep into your eyes and bite my lip I keep fucking you as hard and as fast as I possibly can, you try keeping your eyes locked on mine but every time I touch your g spot you can't keep them from closing and rolling back.. As you scream out my name letting me know I'm fucking you good just the way you like, I begin to lose control and become lost between your thighs, still trapped inside your eyes..

I feel your nails dig in a little deeper on my back and scratch me a little harder as your muscles begin to flex and your body grows tense.. Your legs start to shake, your entire body starts to tremble beneath me and you start to scream out letting me know you're about to cum..

"Fuck Joe, baby I'm gonna fuckin cum.."

Just as you finish your sentence I thrust deep inside you one final time and you release, exploding for me and your cum squirting out from your pussy drenching me in your sweet delicious nectar.. Soaking the bed sheets and making a very big mess for me just the way I like it, your body convulsing and shaking as you make sure to let out every last drop of cum inside your body.. Finally when you finish I feel you relax and sink into the bed a little bit, I let myself fall down beside you and pull you in close to me.. Holding you tight as you breath heavy and your heart races inside your chest, kissing your cheek and rubbing my nose against your skin.. I take one deep breath and relax next to you as we drift off to sleep to fuck some more in our dreams..

41055544R00068

Made in the USA
Charleston, SC
17 April 2015